THE MERMAID AND THE MAJOR

THE TRUE STORY OF THE INVENTION OF THE SUBMARINE

Story and illustrations by
FRANCISCO MELÉNDEZ

Adapted by Robert Morton
from the translation by William Dyckes

Harry N. Abrams, Inc.,
Publishers, New York

MAJOR MICHELANGELO MONDAY was the last member of an ancient family of Spain. The Major had been a soldier most of his life, but he was seldom in battle. He was more interested in inventing things than in waging war.

He had, for example, designed a huge machine for breaking the gates of enemy strongholds. The machine had a long arm that ended in the shape of a roaring lion made of heavy bronze. The lion could swing out of the tower and smash thick wooden doors as if they were made of paper.

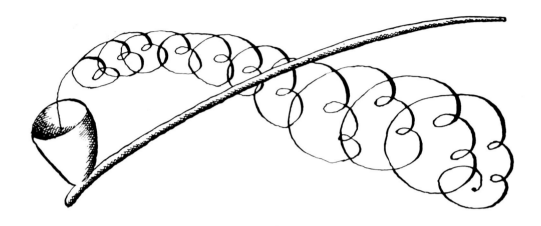

The Major had also devised a mechanical butler to serve his officer colleagues. This automated man had a brain made from a clock and though it couldn't speak, it could walk, move its arms and legs, turn its head, and give a proper military salute.

The butler was programmed to walk every morning across the camp from the kitchen carrying a silver tray with hot chocolate and buttered biscuits for the Commanding General and his senior officers. He did this—even during battles—without spilling a single drop! The General was so impressed that he gave the Major a medal.

Another of the Major's wonderful inventions was a mechanical military marching band. This remarkable device took the place of one hundred sixty-two musicians, who could then carry guns and swords instead of musical instruments. The band featured a hydraulic organ, assorted horns, a string trio, a snare drum, a kettle drum that could play any number of different rhythms, and a stainless steel sackbut—about which I can tell you nothing.

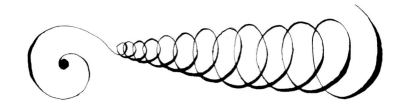

The Major's most powerful weapon was one designed *not* to destroy but to win battles nonetheless. He described it as an "aerial inspiration," and it was used for troops that had lost the will to fight. In every army, you see, a problem arises when one side seems to face certain defeat. The soldiers tend to break ranks and run like frightened mice. Once they begin to flee, it is nearly impossible for officers to persuade them to return to battle. The Major's invention puts an end to all that. As soon as the troops begin to run, the commander-in-chief fires a special rocket that climbs high above the battlefield and explodes with a thundering roar. The sky fills with pictures of the flag and patriotic phrases such as "God save the King!" along with encouraging expressions like "Hurrah, fellows, you're doing well!" All this is produced in brightly colored smoke. Encouraged by this aerial display, the soldiers pick up their rifles and return to battle. More often than not, they win.

There came a time, finally, in the Major's career when the battles ended and the parades ceased. Wars seemed to be a thing of

the past, and the Major found himself with very little to do. So he decided to leave the army and return to his family estate on the shores of the Mediterranean.

He had planned to take with him his mechanical butler. But someone had overwound the clock in the butler's head and one day he just flew to pieces. The Major was very sad to lose his obedient friend, not to mention the hot chocolate and buttered biscuits.

Needing company and a clever helper, the Major asked the General for permission to take with him Corporal Tobias Tuesday. The Corporal was surprisingly well educated for a common soldier. He could read and write, cook several delicious dishes, and was as loyal as three dogs.

Corporal Tuesday was an orphan and appreciated the kindness and generosity of the Major, in addition to admiring his many inventions. He did not always understand these creations but he had a natural talent for mechanical things. And when the Major told him what to do, he had no trouble installing a cog here, a wheel there, or a pulley over there.

The Major was happy to be home. His lovely villa by the sea was a peaceful haven. Now the only sounds that reached his ears—which had been accustomed to the roar of cannons and the crackle of rifles—were the gentle whispers of sea breezes and the voices of birds. His nose soon forgot the smell of gunpowder and his eyes rested on the colorful flowers in his garden.

Most men would have found such beauty putting their minds to sleep. But not the Major.

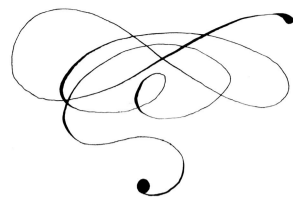

His brain continued to bubble, ideas flowed freely. Still mindful of his former occupation, and unconvinced that war had truly ended for good, he began a careful study of the crab to see if he could make soldiers bulletproof. He thought this might happen if troops were fed a rich crab soup fortified with various irons and minerals. Over a period of months, he reasoned, this would cause a man's skin to become as hard as the shell of a crab.

While the Major studied and wrote, the good Corporal served as butler, barber, cook, and valet. Things continued in this way for some months. Then, one bright August morning, the Major set out to walk the sandy shore and look for crabs for his experiments. As he strolled along he studied the strange shapes of the rocky cliffs above the beach. Their forms reminded him of castles he had seen and he amused himself by imagining where he would place cannons to attack those walls. He paid no attention to what was going on around him. His head was full of towers and trenches and moats and mines.

It was high noon, and the sky was cloudless. The sea looked like liquid fire. The sun shone savagely upon the sand—and upon the head of the Major, who had forgotten this day to wear a hat.

He began to feel dizzy. He paused and wiped his forehead with his handkerchief.

As the Major looked around for a bit of shade, he noticed a strange shape at the edge of the water. It moved very slowly. What could it be? Some brave sailor who had fallen off his ship and been washed ashore?

The Major unbuttoned his vest in order to breathe more easily. As he walked slowly forward, he put his hand over his brow in order to see more clearly. He could not believe his eyes.

The shape was that of a graceful young woman. Her hair was a reddish-blonde color set off by a ribbon and several seashells. It was done up in the style of the Spanish court, although it was not as neatly combed. Her skin was pale gold. And all that she wore was a fishtail and a few strands of seaweed!

The Major felt most uncomfortable. As he approached her, he tried to decide what to do next. He thought he should speak, but he had no idea what to say. In his entire life he had almost never spoken to a young woman alone, and certainly never a woman like this. He shoved his hands in his pockets and then took them out again. He cleared his throat. He felt as if his body was covered with a thousand itches.

He might have spent the rest of the day debating the matter, but as he came near, the young woman looked up at him and smiled. Her teeth were pearly white. Her eyelids fluttered like a pair of purple butterflies.

Then she spoke to him in his own language, although she had a most unusual accent.

She said, "I have often seen you walk along this beach, and I am curious. You are obviously not a fisherman: your face is too pale and your clothing too fine. You walk back and forth along the beach, pointing at the cliffs and talking to yourself. And you collect crabs. Or rather, you try to collect them—for you are not very successful."

"Señorita," said the Major, recovering his savoir-faire, "permit me to introduce myself. My name is Michelangelo Monday, and I am a retired Major of the Royal Imperial Army. You are correct, of course, I am not a fisherman but a student of the sciences. I am presently engaged in a study of the skeletal characteristics of crabs and the potential military applications thereof."

"The what?" she asked.

"The bones of the crab," he explained, "are on the outside of its body, and that is called an exoskeleton."

"But why must you study it?" she said. "All that anyone has to know about crabs is that they taste good. If you are hungry, you pick one up and eat it."

And so saying, she slipped her hand into the water, pulled out a fat red crab, took a big bite as if it was a sandwich, and threw the rest over her shoulder. Spitting out the shell, she said, "That is what crabs are for."

"Now tell me about yourself. You are a strange man, and I want to know more about you."

She laughed a joyful laugh that set her hair shaking in the sunbeams. Dolphins must laugh like that, thought the Major, when they leap and frolic in the sea. And then, suddenly, her expression changed.

"There is something in my eye," she exclaimed. "A piece of shell, perhaps, or a grain of sand. Would you please get it out?"

"Well, yes, of course, it would be a . . . pleasure. Allow me, excuse me, if I may. . . ."

At that moment, Major Monday felt a cold shiver shake his body. He realized that he was more afraid of this young woman than he had been of all the armies he had ever faced. For the first time in his life, he wanted to turn and run away.

Instead, he took out his handkerchief and peered into her eye. He could see neither sand nor shell there, only a large and lovely eye.

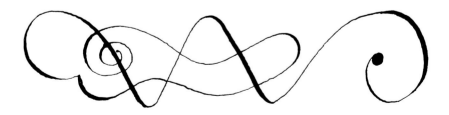

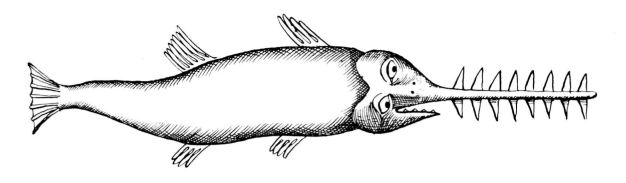

"I can find no foreign objects in your eye, Señorita."

"Look more closely, I beg you! I'm sure it's there, for I feel a most dreadful pain!"

The Major looked deeper into the whirlpool that was her eye—farther and farther, until he forgot who and where he was. Then he felt something new and different, something that he had never felt before.

"What is happening to me?" he wondered. Before he could answer, he found himself drifting into a deep, blue-green pool bordered by eyelashes.

His reverie was interrupted as the young woman suddenly said, "I think you found something," laughing in the same delightful way she had before. "I thank you, sir. Now I must go."

The Major was as shocked as if she had slapped him in the face. He shook his head to clear his mind.

"What is your name, sweet lady?" he asked. "And what exactly are you?"

"I am a mermaid. My name is Maria-Theresa."

"Please forgive my ignorance, dear lady!" begged the Major. "I should have known. Now please tell me: will I have the pleasure of seeing you again?"

She nodded. "I may swim this way again tomorrow at this time. But I cannot stay out of the water for long because my skin gets dry."

"Shall we meet at these rocks?" asked the Major. "Perhaps you would be more comfortable in their shadow."

"Perhaps," said the mermaid, and slipped under the waves.

The Major returned home as quickly as he could. He told Tuesday about his strange encounter on the shore.

Explaining how smitten he was with the young woman, the Major confessed that he did not know how to proceed. The Corporal encouraged him to visit her again. Immediately. Dressed in

his best uniform. And, after making some polite conversation and capturing her heart—to marry her. The Major was convinced.

During the night, Tuesday got out his master's best clothes. He cleaned the coat of blue silk and polished all its buttons until it looked as good as new. The red velvet breeches, it turned out, had been eaten by moths, and so the Corporal had to use the ones made of red plush. The best of the wigs had also suffered. It had been hung upside down for several years and become home for a family of swallows. But it, too, was combed and powdered, made to look like new.

The Major and his man set out for the beach the following morning. They marched side by side like soldiers on parade. The blue coat was as brilliant as the summer sky, and the Corporal's green suit sparkled in the sunshine like the wings of a dragonfly.

As they neared the rocks, the Major began to fret.

"What shall I do if she does not come today?" he asked. "Perhaps we should turn around and go home. Besides, my shoes are full of sand."

"You are not wearing shoes, sir," replied the Corporal. "They are boots, and much too high to let anything in but your feet. Be brave! We have come too far to turn back. There are the rocks at which you are to meet your lady love. I will attend you here."

The Major climbed up onto the rocks and looked around.

"Maria-Theresa!" he whispered. "My dear Maria-Theresa! Are you here? I cannot see you."

In the shadows, someone coughed.

"Ah, there you are!" he said. "I was afraid you had not come."

"I came," said the mermaid. "But I did not realize that this was going to be a costume ball. Why are you all dressed up? And why did you have the ridiculous idea of meeting on these rocks? It does not seem to have occurred to you that people with fishtails have a hard time climbing rocks."

The Major was worried. He had just got there and already she was angry with him. Remembering that Tuesday had said something about jokes, he tried desperately to invent one.

"Then next time I shall bring a ladder," he said, smiling to show that it was a joke.

"Ha!, ha!, and more ha!," replied the mermaid. "That is not very funny."

That did not work at all, thought the Major. Perhaps this would be a good time to try being silent.

But after a few minutes of silence, Maria-Theresa yawned.

"Your silence," she said, "is even more boring than your jokes."

"Forgive me, dear lady," he said, "I was trying to think of the best way to declare my love for you. But I am a man of few words and none of them are much use right now, for I have never spoken of love before."

"Love?" said Maria-Theresa. "Are you not aware, sir, that I am a mermaid and that I live in the sea? You interest me when you are not making jokes or being altogether silent, but that is not enough for love. You walk on land, I swim in the sea. How could we ever be together? Do you wish me to dry up like a salted herring? Or would you rather tell your jokes underwater and drown? There is no place for love in our lives."

Having said that, and nearly broken the poor man's heart, she leaped from the rock and vanished into the sea.

A few days passed. The two men were in the garden. The Major was walking in large, uneven circles, like a man rowing a boat with only one oar.

"Sir," asked the Corporal sadly, "will you never forget her?"

"No," answered the Major. "It would be easier to forget my own name."

"But, sir, she is so thin, so small, so fishy. . . ."

"Such things make no difference to a man in love."

"Sir, in these last few days you have written ninety poems to her. It worries me to see you there, night after night, writing by candlelight. Your skin has begun to turn a strange color, and I am afraid you will become ill. Why not put this energy to better use? Why not invent something?"

"What can I do, my dear Corporal?" asked the Major. "My ears are filled with the sound of her name and I cannot concentrate. How could I invent when I cannot think?"

"It did occur to me, sir, that there is one invention that no man of science has yet devised—a boat that could travel under water. And that would bring you near her."

The Major stopped walking so suddenly that his left foot remained hanging in air. He was so happy that he ran right through the garden pool to embrace his friend.

"Tuesday," he said, laughing and crying at the same time, "most faithful friend! You have found the key to my prison! I shall use my brain to save my heart. I will invent the greatest invention of all time and become the happiest man on Earth!"

The two men danced around the garden, full of the joy that comes with solving the problems that life puts in the way of happiness.

They began by looking for a model for their invention.

They considered many animals that thrive in the water: frogs, swans, eels and octopi, turtles and hermit crabs, seals and shrimp. In the end, they decided to use the fish. "It combines," said the Major, "an elegant simplicity with an exceptional appropriateness."

There were, however, many matters to be resolved.

Should the submarine be constructed *exactly* like a fish? Should it move by wiggling its tail? Or should it have a propeller in the back?

"I am not a young man any longer," said the Major, "and I will soon run out of breath if I have to crank the propeller while under water. Therefore, we will create a motor that uses heat to transform water into steam, thereby generating a great pressure that can be used to turn a propeller!"

Corporal Tuesday suggested that the ship should have two hind legs like a frog, for stability. "For that matter," he added, "two front legs would also be useful for the times when it comes on shore."

There was also the question of how they would move up and down in the water.

Again, it was Tuesday who came up with the solution. He recalled that soldiers with empty stomachs were able to jump much higher than those whose stomachs were full.

"We could put a tank in the boat and fill it with water. When we pump the water out the boat will rise; when we let water in again, the boat will sink."

"Marvelous!" exclaimed the Major. "I swear that I have never had such a good time in my life as I am having right now."

"Nor I, sir," agreed the Corporal.

And they set to work.

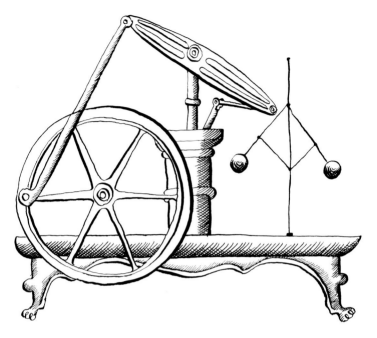

When the steam engine was finally finished, the outside of the boat was already complete. The Corporal had carefully plugged the seams of the ship with rosin and tar, so that not a drop of water could get in. He did it from the inside because he knew that the Major wanted the outside to look as beautiful as possible. It would have a smooth and streamlined skin of steel that shined like the scales of his mermaid.

When they were nearly finished, Tuesday thought of a rather important question:

"How will you be able to breathe while you are under water?"

They immediately stopped work and made a tiny model of the ship. They took it to the pool in the garden and performed a series of experiments. Inside the model they placed a succession of small animals—rats caught in the pantry, garden crickets, and various insects. The Corporal held the boat under water while the Major kept track of the time. They discovered that the crews of these experimental voyages never lasted more than half an hour.

Then the Corporal had another idea: "Suppose we put a sort of chimney on the ship, that you could stick out above the waves from time to time. You

could draw in enough air to fill the ship. Then you would not have to stop."

"You have found the answer!" said the Major.

It took an entire year to complete the submarine. When they were done, as always happens with men who build boats indoors, the ship was too big to fit through the door, so they had to take the workshop apart. And when the walls were down and the ship was uncovered, both men gasped. Their submarine was a wondrous sight, a work of art as well as science: it had the shape of a fat

cigar, and a nose like a dolphin's. Its skin was made of metal and wood. The circular windows in the bow, made of rare Venetian glass, looked like the eyes of a fish. The ship stood upon four legs: two that looked like those of a frog and two that resembled those of a horse. At the back was the propeller and a set of rudders. Crowning the ship was a curved chimney for the intake of air and the exhalation of smoke; it was shaped like the neck of a swan.

When they moved the submarine out of the villa, country people stopped and stared. One thought the ship must be a dragon, another said it was a witch's wagon.

It took the two men several hours to move the ship to the edge of the sea. It was no easy matter.

"Now we must baptize our creation," said the Major. "Every ship in the Royal Imperial Navy has a name of its own, and ours deserves one, too. But what shall we call it?"

"May I suggest, sir, a mythological animal? I speak, of course, of the famous Chimera."

"It has a lovely sound, Tuesday," agreed the Major, "but as I recall, the Chimera had the head of a lion, the body of a goat, and the tail of a snake."

"No matter, sir," responded the Corporal. "Both are a strange collection of beasts."

"Then let us call it that," agreed the Major. "And since you have named it, you may have the honor of writing that name on the bow."

So the Corporal took a bottle of waterproof ink and wrote—in French, of course, for that was the language of romance—*La Chimère*.

While he was doing that, the Major fetched a bottle of champagne. He intended to baptize the ship in the traditional way: by breaking a bottle on the bow.

"Be careful, sir," whispered the Corporal. "If you hit it in the eye, we shall have to wait two more months for another window from Venice."

"Do not worry, Tuesday," replied the Major. "I shall aim well, for I am dying of impatience. I long to see Maria-Theresa so that I may impress her with this demonstration of my love."

He cracked the big black bottle in tiny bits on the nose of the ship and champagne shimmered on its silvery surface. Then the Major climbed inside. When he was halfway in, he turned around and looked back to give a little speech, for that is what one does on such occasions, though here the only audience was Corporal Tuesday.

"I did not build this ship in order to become known as the world's greatest inventor, to earn riches, or for the glory of Spain—but for love of the fair Maria-Theresa, who awaits me under the sea.

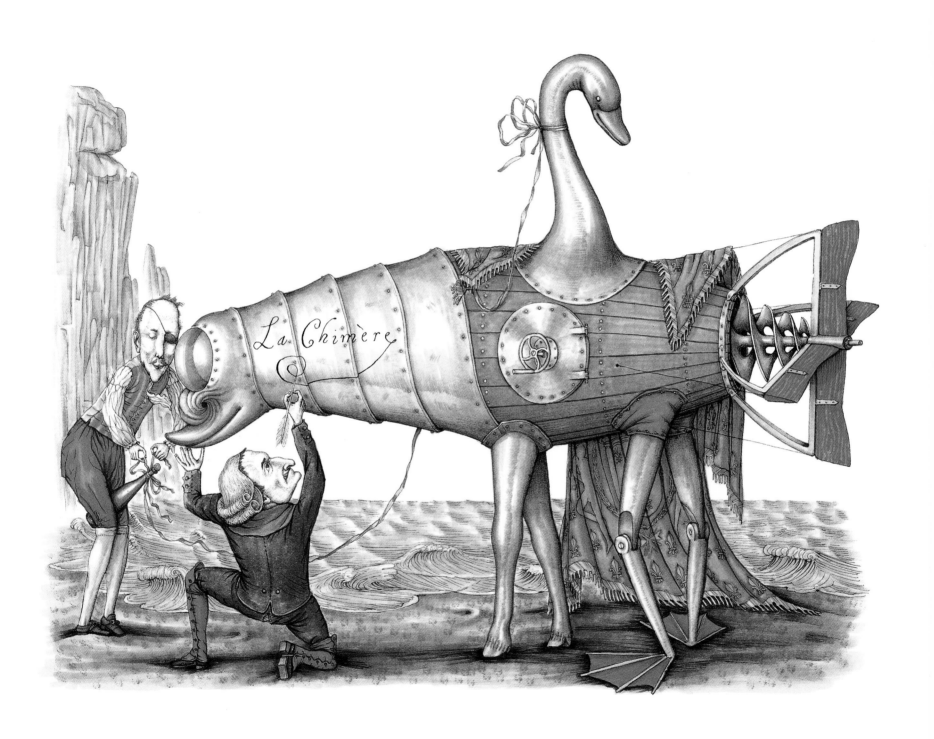

"I shall miss you, dear friend," he said to the Corporal, "but my life is finally about to begin. Farewell."

"Goodbye, your honor," said Tuesday, his eyes wet with tears.

"Goodbye," said the Major, and he pulled in his head and shut the door behind him.

Then the strange ship hop-walked into the water on its frog-horse legs and slipped into the sea. Soon, nothing was heard but the soft lapping of the waves.

As the submarine sank slowly beneath the sea, the Major stared at the strange sights. He had never seen the bottom of the sea. Indeed, he had never been in the sea except to chase crabs in the shallows, and the world he found there was as exotic as the mermaid herself. For a while he moved the wheels and levers that steered the ship, but soon the rhythmic humming of the steam engine began to make him sleepy. He stood up—and hit his head on the low ceiling. He decided to sit on the bed.

It was not long before Maria-Theresa appeared. She did not recognize the Major until he waved to her from the window.

"Theresa, my dear! It is I, your Michelangelo! I could not live without you, so I have come to join you in the sea."

Although Maria-Theresa did not understand the first thing about machines, she was impressed by the wonderful submarine. No one had ever gone to so much trouble for her before.

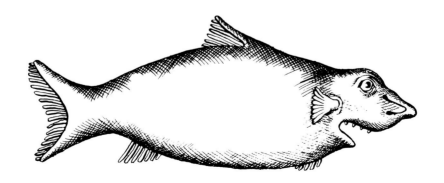

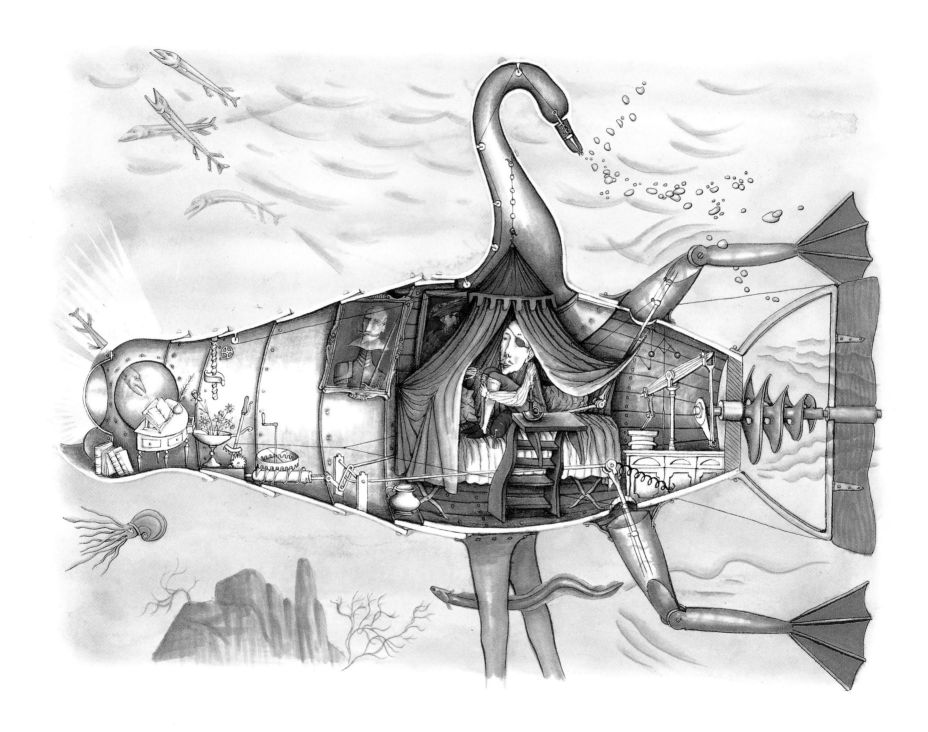

"I never dreamed your devotion was this great," said the lady. "You are indeed worthy of my love."

"Then marry me," said the Major, "and make me the happiest man on Earth—or rather, under water."

"I will," she said, "if my father, the King, will allow it."

And then she kissed him—or rather, she kissed the window, and nearly broke her nose on the glass.

"What is this?" she asked. "Are you locked up in there? Can't you remove this?"

"No," he admitted. "I would not be able to breathe if I did."

"How stupid!" she said. "How are we going to get married if you are locked up inside a tin can?"

"It may not be ideal," allowed the Major, "but it was the best that I could do."

"Well," she replied, "I shall ask my father if he has any ideas."

And she swam off to find him.

When Maria-Theresa returned, she looked unhappy. "My father will not let me marry you," she said.

"But why?" asked the Major.

"He said that it would be foolish for a mermaid to marry a mere man instead of a merman," she answered. "I tried to convince him. If you can find another way to live here, I will marry you, Michelangelo, for you are very amusing. But now I must go. Night is sinking, and I must be in my oyster bed by midnight. *Hasta la vista.*"

It was a dark and bitter night for the Major. He sat in the tiny cabin and stared into space. As the air became stale, he thought of ending it all. "If I cannot live with Maria-Theresa, why should I live at all? I should open the window that separates us and let the murky waters swallow me."

Toward midnight, the Major saw a large fishtail near his window.

Has she returned, he wondered? Is there hope? He ran to the window and looked, but the face that he saw was not that of his beloved. It was a large and ugly fish with round yellow eyes and pointed teeth.

For the next hour, the fish continued to swim nearby. Perhaps the submarine reminded the fish of its mother. The Major sat at his writing desk and stared out the window at the fish. The fish stared back. How fortunate that silly creature is, thought the Major: it lives in the same sea as my beautiful Maria-Theresa. How happily I would trade places with it.

"Why shouldn't I?" he suddenly said out loud. And then he made a decision that would change his life forever.

Back at the villa, it was nearly dawn but Corporal Tuesday had not gone to bed. He sat in the kitchen drinking from a bottle of red wine. "What now?" he wondered. "My master has gone to live under the sea, and I am all alone. No more inventions to be invented, no more books to be written, no more wars to be won. What will I do without the Major?"

As if in answer to his prayers, the door opened and the Major entered. He was soaking wet and carried a large fish over his shoulders.

"Good morning, Corporal," he said, dropping the fish to the floor.

"Good morning, sir," said Tuesday, jumping to his feet and saluting. "What new adventure have we for today?"

The Corporal listened carefully while the Major spoke of his unfortunate experience under the sea. When he explained what he wanted to do next, the Corporal almost fell over.

As it happened, Corporal Tuesday had briefly served during his army career as assistant to the chief surgeon. He had learned how to sew up cuts, cut off legs, cauterize wounds, and all the other little tasks that war demands. Without further ado, he washed his hands, put on a clean smock, boiled some knives and needles, and did what the Major asked.

When the operation was over, and scarcely taking the time to thank Tuesday and bid him farewell, the Major flip-flopped his way out the door of the villa, down the garden path, along the beach, and into the sea.

In the water, when he had become accustomed to wriggling his bottom to move, and still holding his nose until his half-gills had time to work, he swam off to find his love. Here was a brand new world, filled with places of wonder and peopled with amazing creatures. But he was not here to see the sights. He was here to find his lady. Soon he did.

"Maria," he bubbled. "It is I, your Michelangelo, returned to you! There is no ship to separate us. I have become a merman so that I may live with you under the sea."

"How handsome you are in your silver tail," she exclaimed. "How brave you are to have done this! Now my father will have to let us marry."

All the pain that the Major had suffered was erased the instant he heard those words.

Hailing a friendly whale, the loving couple rode off on its back to the court of the King. There, the Major was introduced to Maria's father. He met her two imperious sisters and a not-very-friendly younger brother. It seemed that this family into which he was marrying was not delighted with their new member. The King, in particular, showed his disdain for the newcomer. He looked down his long and narrow nose, barely able to contain his displeasure. But the King knew that if he refused her wishes, his daughter might do something even more foolish.

So the Princess and her gallant Major were married.

In the months that followed, Maria-Theresa showed the Major her world, and it was more beautiful than he had ever imagined. He saw how the light filtered down from the surface and how it danced, twisting and turning in the water, leaping off rocks and shells in cascades of color. He watched schools of tiny fish slip through the transparent water, turning left and right as if they were a single animal. An octopus waved to them with all

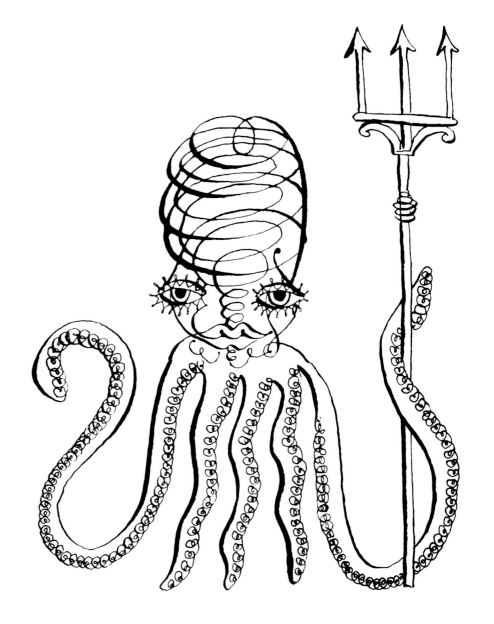

eight legs. Mermaids giggled behind a curtain of colored coral. Green crabs scurried across the white sand. And all the while, a mysterious, crystalline music reached his ears, a music more beautiful than any he had ever heard.

Maria-Theresa showed him the Royal Garden, with its bountiful beds of sea flowers. Soon he had seen all there was to see, and the Major and his mermaid settled down to everyday life.

It soon became clear, however, that their life was no bed of pearls. There were problems. The princess's sisters and other members of the royal court treated the Major as if he were some rare animal in a zoo. They stared and wouldn't speak to him. Each time he met the King he was expected to say how much better life was under water. (Which he did not think was true.) Maria-Theresa spent much of her time playing tricks on him. Once, when the Major was trying to write a letter to Corporal Tuesday, the mermaid replaced his waterproof ink with the ink of an octopus. Not a word remained on the paper. Several times she interrupted his study of crabs by eating all of his subjects.

Life together became more and more difficult. In time, they rarely agreed on anything.

"Darling," Maria-Theresa might say, "I want to go to the Aquatic Ballet tonight."

"I am sorry, my love," the Major might reply, "but I have some crab study to do. I have not paid enough attention to my research lately."

"But what will my friends think if you don't go?"

"Tell them the truth," he would reply.

"I know what they will think!" she would shout. "They will think that I am ashamed to be seen with you because you are only a human."

"And what is wrong with being a human?" asked the Major.

"You breathe air. When we *do* go to the theater, you are forever swimming off to the surface."

"Well, there is nothing I can do about that," replied the Major.

"If you loved me, you would live without air," she shouted.

"Let's not argue," said the Major.

"The worst part," she insisted, "is that you would rather spend your time with nasty little crabs than with me!"

"It was a mistake to marry you," she told him one day. "My father warned me, but I didn't listen. My friends warned me, too. Now look what has happened."

"Your father," said the Major, "has the brains of fish as well as the body of one. And your friends know nothing at all! They have no other interests than to chew on crabs and talk about seahorse racing. If I were still on land, I'd catch the lot of them and fry them up for supper!"

This argument was only the first, but many followed, and gradually their passion grew as cold as the deep ocean water. Maria-Theresa took to flirting with a huge, horned sea-world centaur, and not just to make the Major jealous.

Finally, he could stand it no longer.

He swam to the surface for a breath of air . . . and never returned.

On the shore and no longer able to walk, the Major had to drag himself up the hill and into his garden. When he got there, the house seemed different. Have I been away so long? he asked himself. Is it just the darkness?

But then he began to notice changes. In place of the magnificent beds of flowers, the garden was filled with a random assortment of onions, lettuce, and other vegetables. The house had not been kept up. It was badly in need of painting and several of the shutters had fallen off. Where, he wondered, was Corporal Tuesday?

"Pssst! Sir, over here," someone whispered from the shadows.

"Tuesday? Is that you? What is wrong?"

"Quickly, sir, you must hide," said the voice.

The Major pulled himself through the fallen leaves to the place where the Corporal was hiding.

"Tuesday! What are you doing here? Why haven't you shaved? Why are you dressed in rags?"

"Many things have happened, sir. While you were among the sardines, there was a revolution. The people rose up and killed the King. They took over your house and lands. I have been forced to work as a gardener, but I remained nearby to see if you would return."

"But what about my books, my inventions?" asked the Major.

"Sir, everything is burned, broken, stolen, sold, or destroyed."

This was a calamity. But the Major was a soldier. Defeat was not in his vocabulary. Realizing that they must quickly depart, he asked Tuesday to find a wheelbarrow to carry him in. Soon they were trundling down the road toward the city. Where they would go and what they would do they did not know.

Next day, as they stopped to rest at a busy street corner, Tuesday placed the Major on the ground while he went off to hide the wheelbarrow. When he returned he found that passersby had dropped some money in the hat that he had left on the ground in front of the Major.

Here was their salvation. Now they were able to earn a living. Thus, on the street corners of the towns, among the jesters and jugglers and beggars who performed there, they exhibited the Major, announcing him as a triton from the far-off islands of Greece. The Major confounded the gawking crowds by addressing them in ancient Greek. Since they didn't understand anything that he said he often told them how stupid and ugly they were. They simply laughed at the strange words. Corporal Tuesday played a little mechanical hand organ and asked the crowd for money. The forlorn pair earned enough to live on.

So they continued, day by day.

Tuesday dreamed of the glory times in the Army. The Major retreated in his thoughts to the world of invention. Again he pondered how he could make soldiers impervious to bullets. The crab solution seemed imperfect, but perhaps there was something more interesting to be done with a wheelbarrow. Suppose one turned it over, made it larger and put wheels on it; then troops could huddle beneath it for protection from the enemy's fire. Perhaps, perhaps, perhaps . . .

His submarine, he thought, had been a great device, but no one now would believe that he had made it, and anyway, what use could it be if one were trapped inside, unable to kiss a mermaid or make contact in any way with the undersea world? Still, it had been a wonderful invention and he was determined to find others.

From time to time he thought again of his reckless attempt to live beneath the sea. He tried to make sense of it all. Was his love of the mermaid never meant to be? Had he been foolish to believe that a man could leave his natural element to follow his heart? Were we all confined to the worlds of our births, or could we dream of other realms?

Quien sabe? Who knows?

What we do know is that Michelangelo Monday, true inventor of the submarine, fell in love
—and could not climb out again.

Editor: Robert Morton
Designer: Darilyn Lowe

Library of Congress Catalog Card Number: 91–9273
ISBN 0-8109-3619-4

Copyright © 1989, 1991 Francisco Meléndez
English-language edition copyright © 1991 Harry N. Abrams, Inc.

Published in 1991 by Harry N. Abrams, Incorporated, New York
A Times Mirror Company
Printed and bound in Japan